HAPPY HONEY

THE BEST FALL OF ALL

HAPPY HONEY

THE BEST FALL OF ALL

written by Laura Godwin
pictures by Jane Chapman

SCHOLASTIC INC.
New York Toronto London Auckland Sydney
Mexico City New Delhi Hong Kong Buenos Aires

For the children at the Marigold School in Victoria, B.C.
—L. G.

For Olivia and Georgie
—J. C.

No part of this publication may be reproduced, stored in a retrieval system, or transmitted in any form or by any means, electronic, mechanical, photocopying, recording, or otherwise, without written permission of the publisher. For information regarding permission, write to Simon & Schuster Books for Young Readers, an imprint of Simon & Schuster Children's Publishing Division, 1230 Avenue of the Americas, New York, NY 10020.

ISBN-13: 978-0-545-12135-4
ISBN-10: 0-545-12135-3

Text copyright © 2002 by Laura Godwin.
Illustrations copyright © 2002 by Jane Chapman.
All rights reserved. Published by Scholastic Inc., 557 Broadway, New York, NY 10012, by arrangement with Simon & Schuster Books for Young Readers, an imprint of Simon & Schuster Children's Publishing Division. READY-TO-READ is a registered trademark of Simon & Schuster, Inc. SCHOLASTIC and associated logos are trademarks and/or registered trademarks of Scholastic Inc.

12 11 10 9 8 7 6 5 4 15 16 17 18 19/0

Printed in the U.S.A. 40

First Scholastic printing, October 2008

The text of this book was set in Century Schoolbook.
The illustrations were rendered in acrylic.

Fall is here.
Happy is happy.
Happy likes fall.

Woof, woof.

Happy goes out.

Meow, meow.

Honey goes out.

Honey likes fall too.

Honey sees birds.

She sees
apples and pumpkins.

She sees fall leaves.
She sees fall leaves fall.

Meow, meow.

Honey feels the wind.

The wind is cold.

Honey does not like
the wind.

Woof, woof.

Here comes Happy.

Happy is warm.

Happy likes the wind.

Happy will help Honey
get warm too.

Woof, woof.

Happy runs.

Meow, meow.

Honey runs too.

Happy and Honey
run fast.

They run fast
past the birds.
They run fast
past the pumpkins.

They run fast and
FALL
into the leaves.

What fun!

Then Happy and Honey
run home.

Woof, woof.
Meow, meow.
Happy and Honey
go in.

Now Honey is warm
and happy.
Like Happy.

And Happy is warm
and happy.
Like Honey.

Happy and Honey
fall asleep.

This is the best
fall of all.